Mousekin's Family

Mousekin's Family

story and pictures by EDNA MILLER

PRENTICE-HALL, Inc., Englewood Cliffs, N.J.

To Teddy

Library of Congress Catalog Card Number 69-12673

Printed in the United States of America   ISBN: 0-13-604462-X
                                             ISBN: 0-13-604157-4 (pbk.)

20   19   18   17   16   15

Lightning streaked through the forest.
Thunder rolled in the hills.
Mousekin darted under a burdock leaf
to keep the rain away.

From beneath his leafy umbrella,
Mousekin could see his home
in the branches of the wild cherry tree.
He had been away from his nest
for a short mousetime...
for as long as it takes
a pink baby mouse
to grow a coat
of soft grey fur
and leave the warmth
of its mother's side.
It was Mousekin's turn now
to watch over his young
as they learned how to live in the forest.

While he waited for the rain to stop falling,
Mousekin busily nibbled fruit
blown from a nearby tree.
He never even noticed the stranger
that shared his leaf in the storm
until he felt something furry
snuggle close beside him.

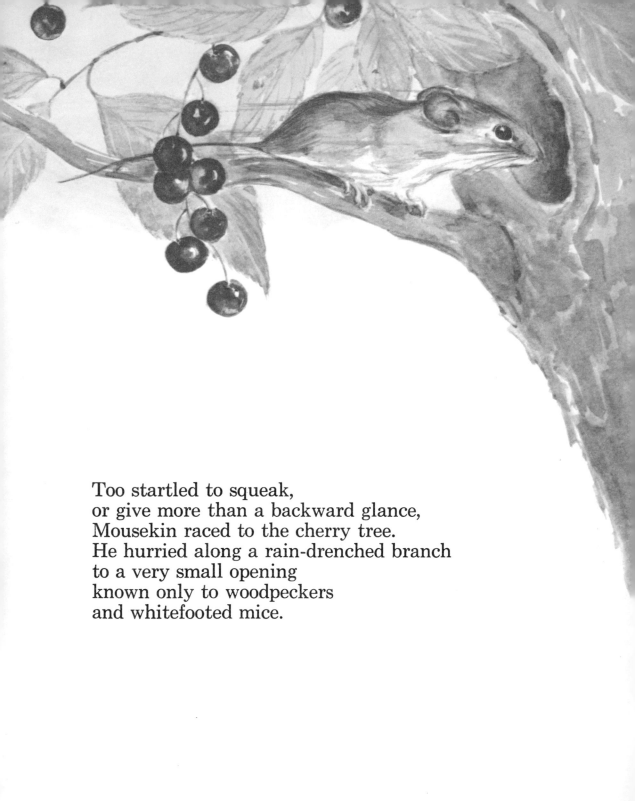

Too startled to squeak,
or give more than a backward glance,
Mousekin raced to the cherry tree.
He hurried along a rain-drenched branch
to a very small opening
known only to woodpeckers
and whitefooted mice.

There were no sounds
of baby mice at play
inside the down-filled hollow.
Mousekin's nest was empty.
As he turned to search for his family,
Mousekin heard a twittering call.

Far below, in firefly light,
stood the strange creature
Mousekin had glimpsed
under the burdock leaf.
It had small mouse eyes,
small mouse ears,
tiny mouse paws
with hind legs much longer than his own.
Perhaps it was one of his mouselings
that had strayed from the cherry tree nest.
Mousekin gave a welcoming squeak,
calling the little mouse home.

The furry form sat quietly
and seemed not to hear.

Mousekin whistled and squeaked again.
A mouse must *always* come when called!
He drummed his paw upon a branch,
coaxing the baby to climb.
Whitefoot mice *must* learn to climb
to live alone in a forest!
The mouse baby never looked up.

Mousekin skittered down the wild cherry tree
and gently nudged the little creature.
He turned and ran lightly from stone to stone
until he came to the hickory tree.
The mouseling bounded beside him
in great long leaps.

Perhaps his squirrel cousins
could teach the mouse to climb...
for there is no safer place
than some craggy tree hollow
when a whitefoot mouse must hide.

The squirrels chattered noisily
leaping from tree to tree
where branches barely met.
But the baby didn't stop to watch
the racing and chasing far above him.
He leaped in higher and wider circles
beneath the hickory tree.

If the little mouse wouldn't climb,
then he must learn to build a safe home
upon the ground.
Mousekin scrambled here and there
gathering moss and grasses,
tucking them all carefully
beneath a ledge of stone.
A porcupine cousin,
safe within his coat of quills,
watched Mousekin as he worked . . .
but the dainty jumper skipped about
and never turned his head.

Mousekin shuddered as he heard
the wailing call of the screech owl
and the answering bark of a fox.
He knew what could happen to any small mouse
without a home in the forest!

Perhaps his beaver cousins
could teach the mouse to build.
There is no stronger home
than a beaver's lodge
when an owl and a fox are near.

Mousekin hurried to the stream
with the jumper close beside him.
Far upstream they could hear splashing
and sharp slapping sounds upon the water.

They peered into the night
as far as mice can see.

Mousekin watched his beaver cousins work...
gnawing and whittling around a tree
until it fell upon the shore.
He watched them float the branches
out to their log-filled homes
and listened as they slapped the water
with broad, flat tails
to signal their going and coming.

But the only thing the naughty jumper saw
was a great hawk moth.
He chased the insect up and down
along the stony bank.
Mousekin heard a turtle sigh
as it drew inside its shell.
The little mouse would never learn
to build a home by *watching*.

But there were other lessons to be learned.
A mouse must know when it is time
to gather and to store
and when it is time to eat the fruit
as it ripens in the sun.
Mousekin turned a blackberry
around and around in his paws.
His whiskers twitched with mousey pleasure.
The baby mouse sat quietly,
looking straight ahead,
not touching the food which Mousekin placed
so temptingly beside him.

Suddenly, the mouseling sprang—

He flew past the blackberry bush.

He flew past a chipmunk
eating an early meal.
With one long leap
the mouseling jumped into a burrow.

But the chipmunk cousin didn't want
an uninvited guest.
The air was filled with squeaks
and squeals and angry scolding.
The little mouse scrambled back
up through the chipmunk doorway.

The little creatures barely heard
a woodchuck cousin's warning whistle—
A hungry hawk was circling high
watching the scene below.

Mousekin scrambled quickly
into the nearest tree
and hid beneath broad leaves.
The chipmunk darted into its burrow,
pushing leaves and dirt up tight
against the entranceway.
... but the little jumper sat alone
in the middle of the clearing.

As the hawk swooped low for its tiny prey,
a large jumping mouse bounded forward
and snatched her baby in a gentle grip.

In one swift motion, both mother and baby
disappeared into the deep shadows
of the underbrush.
Mousekin knew then
that the strange little creature
was a cousin
and not one of his own.

For what seemed like a very long time
Mousekin sat quietly in the tall grass.
The wind blew and a long, low rumble of thunder
broke the stillness once again.
A drop of rain slid past him.

Mousekin turned to search the woods
for a family all his own.
Three whitefoot mice with whitefoot ways
were waiting somewhere for him.
He hurried along familiar paths
back to the wild cherry tree...
and the patter of rain, like tiny mouse feet,
followed him into the forest.